HOW TO:

PERFORM WUDU

&

PRAY

for Muslim Men & Women & kids

In the Name of Allah, the Most Gracious and the Most Merciful

"اللَّهُمَّ صَلِّ عَلَى مُحَمَّدٍ , وَعَلَى آلِ مُحَمَّدٍ , كَمَا صَلَّيْتَ عَلَى إِبْرَاهِيمَ وَعَلَى آلِ إِبْرَاهِيمَ , إِنَّكَ حَمِيدٌ مَجِيدٌ."

"Allahoumma Salli 'ala Muhammadin Wa 'ala Ali Muhammadin, kama Sallita 'ala Ibrahima Wa 'ala ali Ibrahima, Innaka Hamidun Majid"

"O Allah! Send Your Salawat (Graces, Honours and Mercy) on Muhammed and on The family of Muhammed, as You send Your Salawat on Ibrahim and on the family of Ibrahim, for You are The Most Praiseworthy, The Most Glorious "

بِسْمِ اللَّهِ الرَّحْمَنِ الرَّحِيمِ

قَالَ اللَّهُ تَعَالَى :
"فَإِذَا قَضَيْتُمُ الصَّلَاةَ فَاذْكُرُوا اللَّهَ قِيَامًا
وَقُعُودًا وَعَلَىٰ جُنُوبِكُمْ ۚ فَإِذَا اطْمَأْنَنْتُمْ فَأَقِيمُوا
الصَّلَاةَ ۚ إِنَّ الصَّلَاةَ كَانَتْ عَلَى الْمُؤْمِنِينَ
كِتَابًا مَوْقُوتًا" صَدَقَ اللَّهُ الْعَظِيمُ

"When ye pass (Congregational) prayers, celebrate Allah's praises, standing, sitting down, or lying down on your sides; but when ye are free from danger, set up Regular Prayers: For such prayers are enjoined on believers at stated times."

Preface

We are honored and blessed to have authored this *'Learn to perform wudu and pray guide'* in order to help and simplify the process of learning how to perform wudu and pray. We ask Allah u to continue pouring His blessings upon this project and make your path to learn how to pray, filled with light and ease. *"Ameen"*

The instructions and steps in this book are designed for both males and females wanting to learn how to pray.

We understand and respect that there are differences in opinions in relation to certain actions in the prayer, however we chose not to include them in the book in order to simplify the learning process.

The sole purpose of this book is to teach the *basics of prayer*, once you have learnt the foundations of prayer and wish to seek further knowledge, we encourage you to *approach your local Mosque or Islamic Centre* who can assist you with the guidance of the Qur'an and Sunnah of our beloved Prophet "s".

The Salah (Prayer) الصَّلَاةُ

THE IMPORTANCE OF PRAYER:

Salah (Prayer) is one of the fundamental pillars of Islam. It was the first act of worship that was made obligatory by Allah and it is the last thing to be taken away from the religion. When it perishes, Islam will perish.

Its obligation was revealed directly to the Prophet, during his ascension to the heaven and it was made obligatory upon every sane, adult* Muslim. Salah is the first action that a believer will be questioned about, for the Messenger of Allah ﷺ said:

"The first act that the slave will be accountable for on the Day of Judgement will be prayer. If it is good, then the rest of his acts will be good. And if it is deficient, then the rest of his acts will be deficient".

"إِنَّ أَوَّلَ مَا يُحَاسَبُ بِهِ الْعَبْدُ يَوْمَ الْقِيَامَةِ مِنْ عَمَلِهِ صَلَاتُهُ فَإِنْ صَلُحَتْ فَقَدْ أَفْلَحَ وَأَنْجَحَ وَإِنْ فَسَدَتْ فَقَدْ خَابَ وَخَسِرَ فَإِنِ انْتَقَصَ مِنْ فَرِيضَتِهِ شِيءٍ قَالَ الرَّبُّ تَبَارَكَ وَتَعَالَى: انْظُرُوا هَلْ لِعَبْدِي مِنْ تَطَوُّعٍ؟ فَيَكْمُلُ بِهَا مَا انْتَقَصَ مِنَ الْفَرِيضَةِ ثُمَّ يَكُونُ سَائِرُ عَمَلِهِ عَلَى ذَلِكَ) رَوَاهُ التِّرْمِذِي

**Please refer to page 9 for who is considered an adult*

The importance of Salah is so great that one is ordered to observe it in all occasions, whether one is healthy or sick, whether one prays standing, sitting or lying down, whether one is traveling or residing and whether one is safe or in fear. Salah is our key to success in this world and in the hereafter. Allah says in His Glorious Book;

"Successful indeed are the believers who are humble in their prayers" and in another verse "

(alMu'minun: 1-2)

"قَدْ أَفْلَحَ الْمُؤْمِنُونَ الَّذِينَ هُمْ فِي صَلَاتِهِمْ خَاشِعُونَ" (المؤمنون الاية 1-2)

And who pay heed to their prayers. These are the heirs who will inherit Paradise. There will they abide "

(alMu'minun: 9-11)

"وَالَّذِينَ هُمْ عَلَىٰ صَلَوَاتِهِمْ يُحَافِظُونَ أُولَٰئِكَ هُمُ الْوَارِثُونَ الَّذِينَ يَرِثُونَ الْفِرْدَوْسَ هُمْ فِيهَا خَالِدُونَ" (المؤمنون الآية 9-11)

The main purpose of this booklet is to help you learn how to pray correctly as taught to us by the Prophet Muhammad . It provides a simplified, illustrated step-by-step guide to 'Purification & Prayer' which we hope will get you up and running quickly.

THE DEFINITION OF SALAH (PRAYER)

The Arabic word Salah originates from the word silah which means connection.

The Islamic definition of Salah is the name given to the formal prayer of Islam. The prayer is one of the obligatory rites of the religion, to be performed five times a day by every obedient adult* Muslim. It is a connection between the human and their Creator Allah.

The prayers are a type of purification for a human being. They turn and meet with their Lord five times a day. This repeated standing in front of Allah should keep the person from performing sins during the day.

Furthermore, it should also be a time of remorse and repentance, such that they earnestly ask Allah for forgiveness for those sins that they committed. In addition, the prayer in itself is a good deed that wipes away some of the evil deeds that they performed.

---

*Please refer to page 9 for who is considered an adult

These points can be noted in the following hadith of the Prophet ﷺ :

"If a person had a stream outside their door and they bathed in it five times a day, do you think they would have any filth left on them?"
The people said, *"No filth would remain on them whatsoever."* The Prophet then said, *"That is like the five daily prayers: Allah wipes away the sins by them."* (Recorded by al-Bukhari and Muslim.)

One of the Saliheen was asked how he kept his khushu' in prayer (concentration & humbleness etc) He said, 'I imagine that Allah is before me, that the Angel of Death is at my back, that the gardens of Jannah are to my right, that the fires of Jahannum are on my left and that I am standing on the Sirat'

THE 2ND PILLAR OF ISLAM

Salah is the second pillar of Islam. Performing Salah is the first priority after belief in the Oneness of Allah and in the prophethood of Muhammad. It is such an important pillar, that Muslims are called upon to perform this act of worship in all circumstances without fail.

Prayer Tip – Prayer is a protection for you

"Verily, the prayer keeps one from the great sins and evil deeds" (Surah al-Ankaboot 45).

قال الله تعالى :"اتْلُ مَا أُوحِيَ إِلَيْكَ مِنَ الْكِتَاب وَأَقِم الصَّلَاةَ إِنَّ الصَّلَاةَ تَنْهَىٰ عَنِ الْفَحْشَاءِ وَالْمُنْكَرِ وَلَذِكْرُ اللَّهِ أَكْبَرُ وَاللَّهُ يَعْلَمُ مَا تَصْنَعُونَ "
(سورة العنكبوت الآية 45)

This effect has been described in the following eloquent way – "Its aim is to generate within the subliminal self of man such spiritual ، light of faith and awareness of God as can enable him to strive successfully against all kinds of evils and temptations and remain steadfast at times of trial and adversity and protect himself against the weakness of the flesh and the mischief of immoderate appetites." (Nadwi)

Prayer Tip - Prayer is cleansing:

In another hadith, the Prophet ﷺ said, ***"The five daily prayers and the Friday Prayer until the Friday prayer are expiation for what is between them."***

(Recorded by Muslim.)

عَنْ أَبِي هُرَيرَة ـرَضِي اللَّهُ عَنْهُ ـ عَنْ رَسُولِ اللَّه ـصَلَى اللَّهُ عَلَيْهِ وَسَلَّمَ ـ قَالَ: ((الصَّلَوَاتُ الْخَمْسُ، وَالْجُمُعَةُ إِلَى الْجُمُعَةِ، وَرَمَضَانُ إِلَى رَمَضَانِ مُكَفِّرَاتٌ لِمَا بينهنَّ إذا اجتُنبت الْكَبَائِرِ)). (رواه مسلم)

WHO MUST PRAY?:

Prayer is obligatory upon every sane adult Muslim. A person is considered an adult upon reaching puberty. There are four signs of puberty (any one of these signs means the person has reached puberty)

1. *Wet dreams*
2. *Pubic hair*
3. *Menstruation (for girls)*
4. *Reaching the age of 15*

Prayer Tip - Missed Prayers:

It is a ***major sin*** to miss a prayer deliberately; the missed prayer must be made up as soon as it is remembered. Any made-up prayer is performed in the exact manner it is prayed during it's specified time.

The Names and Times of the 5 Daily Prayers

FAJR : *Dawn Prayer*

Fajr : is performed after dawn and before sunrise. Fajr consists of 2 Units (raka'ah).

DHUHR : *Noon Prayer*

Dhuhr : is performed when the sun passes the meridian. Dhuhr consists of 4 Units (raka'ah).

ASR : *Afternoon Prayer*

Asr : is performed midway between noon and sunset. Asr consits of 4 Units (raka'ah).

MAGHREB : *Sunset Prayer*

Maghreb : is performed immediately after sunset. Maghreb consists of 3 Units (raka'ah).

ISHA : *Night Prayer*

Isha : is performed after twilight up until fajr although it is preferred to be prayed before midnight. Isha consists of 4 units (raka'ah).

Prayer Tip - Pray on Time

Remember, it is best to perform each of the five obligatory prayers as soon as the time has commenced, as it is not permitted to delay them without a valid reason, and it must not be delayed beyond its permitted time.

Compulsory (Fard) & Non- Compulsory Prayers (Sunnah)

The following are the number of compulsory and sunnah units associated with each prayer. The highlighted boxes are obligatory. The sunnah prayers are highly recommended, and the person will receive great reward for performing them – however no sin is incurred for skipping them.

Prayer	Before (sunnah)	Compulsory	After (sunnah)
Fajr	2	2 *	_____
Dhuhr	2 + 2	4	2 or (2 + 2)
Asr	2 + 2	4	_____
Maghrib	2	3 *	2
Isha'	2	4 *	2

UmmHabeebah, the wife of the Prophet ﷺ said:
"I heard the Messenger of Allah say: 'There is no Muslim slave who prays twelve rak'ahs to Allah each day, voluntarily, apart from the obligatory prayers, but Allah will build for him a house in Paradise." (TIRMIDHI)

Prayer Tip – Using Prayer Calendars

It is advised that you refer to an *Islamic prayer timetable* published by one of the local Islamic centres in your city for exact time prayers throughout the year. Or download reputable Prayer Apps to provide you with the correct prayer times for your location.

---

*The Qur'anic recitation of the first two units of each of these prayers which have the asterisk besides them should be read aloud All other units of these prayers and other prayers should be recited silently.

*For women, the first 2 units should *only* be read aloud if the person is:
1. leading other women (only) in prayer
2. praying by herself at home / in a private area

Purification & Cleanliness (Tahaarah)

After successfully completing this module you'll be able to:

1. *Know the importance of purification in Islam*
2. *Understand how to perform the ritual actions of wudu*
3. *Determine which actions break or nullify the wudu*

Purification is a very important matter in Islam. One must purify their intention for Allah alone and purify their bodies and clothes before beginning the Prayer.

Hygiene and cleanliness are very important aspects of a Muslim's life. One must ensure that their bodies, clothing and place of prayer is free from impurities such as urine, faeces and any other impure substances.

After going to the toilet, it is compulsory to wash the private parts with water if it is available and does not cause harm (due to injury for example).

It is obligatory to have a full shower known as Ghusl after intimate relations between the husband and wife, after ejaculation by the man (due to a wet dream, for example), and upon completion of a woman's menses or post-natal bleeding.

In the Glorious Quran، Allah ﴾u﴿ states:

"Truly، Allah loves those who turn unto Him in repentance and He loves those who purify themselves"

AL- BAQARAH: 222

قال الله تعالى :

"إِنَّ اللَّهَ يُحِبُّ التَّوَّابِينَ وَيُحِبُّ الْمُتَطَهِّرِينَ" سَوْرَةُ الْبَقَرَةِ الآيَةُ: 222

Wudu' Foundations

THE IMPORTANCE OF WUDU:

The Prophet Muhammad ﷺ said:
"Salah (prayer) of anyone of you who has invalidated his/her purification is not accepted unless he/she makes wudu''. (Bukhari)

THE VIRTUES OF WUDU':

The Prophet Muhammad ﷺ said: "When the Muslim or believing servant performs ablution and washes his/her face, each sin he/she has committed by his/ her eyes washes away with the water. When he/she washes his/her hands, each sin his/her hands have committed washes away with the water – or with the last drop of water until he/she becomes free of sin." (Malik and others).

BEFORE DOING WUDU':

1. *Go to the toilet first (if required). You should use the toilet and then wash the private parts before performing wudu'.*

2. *It is good practice to clean the teeth with siwak (toothstick) or a toothbrush before performing wudu' as taught by the Prophet Muhammad.*

3. *Before starting the actions of wudu', it is necessary to make your intention of washing to be for the purpose of wudu' only.*

How to Perform Wudu' (Step-by-Step)

THE FOLLOWING STEPS MUST BE OBSERVED IN ORDER (TARTEEB).

Step 1 - Bismillah

BEFORE WUDU': Intention of making wudu' should be done in the heart, then say:

(Bismillah (In the name of Allah

بِسْمِ اللَّهِ

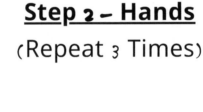

Step 2 - Hands
(Repeat 3 Times)

Completely wash the hands, including the wrists and between the fingers

<u>Step 3 – Mouth</u>
Repeat 3 Times

Rinse the mouth. Using the right hand put a small amount of water into the mouth, swirl around, then expel.

<u>Step 4 – Nose</u>
Repeat 3 Times

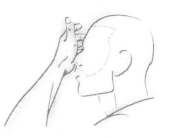

Sniff water into the nostrils as far as possible with the right hand, and then sniff it out with left hand.

<u>*Step 5 – Face*</u>
Repeat 3 Times

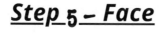

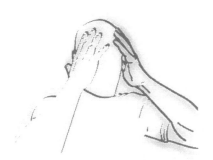

Wash the face from forehead to chin, left earlobe to the right earlobe making sure the whole face is washed.

Step 6 – Arms

Repeat 3 Times

Wash the two arms up to and including the elbows, hand and between the fingers.
Begin with the right arm.

Step 7 – Head

Wipe the head with wet fingers starting at the fringe to the back hairline and back the same way all in one movement.

Step 8 – Ears

Simultaneously wipe the insides of both ears with index finger, and the back of the ears with the thumbs

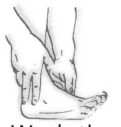

Step ٩– Feet

Repeat ٣ Times

Wash the feet including the ankles and between the toes. Begin with the right foot.

Step ١٠ – Closing Du'a/Invocation

AFTER WUDU': Say:

Ash-hadu anllaa ilaaha illallaah wa ash-hadu anna Muhammadan 'abduhu wa rasooluh

(I bear witness that there is no God worthy of worship except Allah. And I bear witness that Muhammad is His slave and Messenger.)

"أَشْهَدُ أَنْ لَا إِلَهَ إِلَّا اللَّهُ وَأَشْهَدُ أَنَّ مُحَمَّدًا عَبْدُهُ وَرَسُولُهُ"

and:

Allahuma ij-'alnee minat-tawabeen waj-'alnee minalmutatahireen

Oh Allah, make me among those who turn in repentance to you and make me among those who purify themselves

"اللَّهُمَّ اجْعَلْنِي مِنَ التَّوَّابِينَ ، واجْعَلْنِي مِنَ المُتَطَهِّرِينَ"

Actions which Nullify the Wudu

The following actions nullify the Wudu – i.e. it has to be performed again in order to pray. These are in regards to both men and women:

1. *Passing wind.*
2. *Passing urine or faeces*
3. *Full mouth vomiting*
4. *Flowing of blood or pus from any part of the body.*
5. *Deep sleep, whereby one loses awareness.*
6. *Unconsciousness or intoxication*
7. *Touching the private parts with the hand and fingers without a barrier.*
8. *Intimate relations ***

The Prophet Muhammad ﷺ said:
"Whoever performs Wudu' well then says, (the mentioned supplication); the eight gates of Paradise will be opened for him to enter through any one he wills."

(muslim)

---

*It is mandatory for a person to take a full bath/ shower after having intimate relations with their husband/ wife in order to be in a state of purity for prayer.

قَالَ رَسُولُ اللَّهِ ـ صَلَّى اللَّهُ عَلِيهِ وَسَلَّمَ :

" إِسْبَاغُ الْوُضُوءِ شَطْرُ الإِيمَانَ وَالْحَمْدُ لِلّهِ تَمْلأُ الْمِيزَانَ وَالتَّسْبِيحُ وَالتَّكْبِيرُ مِلْءُ السَّمَوَاتِ وَالأَرْض وَالصَّلاَةُ نُورٌ وَالزَّكَاةُ بُرْهَانٌ وَالصَّبْرُ ضِيَاءٌ وَالْقُرْآنُ حُجَّةٌ لَكَ أَوْ عَلَيْكَ كُلُّ النَّاسِ يَغْدُو فَبَائِعٌ نَفْسَهُ فَمُعْتِقُهَا أَوْ مُوبِقُهَا " .

The Messenger of Allah ﷺ said:

"Performing ablution properly is half of faith, saying Al-Hamdu Lillah fills the Scale (of good deeds), saying Subhan-Allah and Allahu Akbar fills the heavens and the earth, prayer is light, Zakat is proof, patience is brightness and the Qur'an is proof for you or against you. Every person goes out in the morning to sell his soul, so he either frees it or destroys it.'

(Sunan Ibn Majah)

Wudu Tip - Forgetfullness

If a person forgets whether they have nullified their wudu' or not, **then this does NOT nullify their ablution,** regardless of whether the person is praying or not, until they are certain that they have nullified their ablution.

Wudu Tip - Menstruation

A menstruating or post natal woman **must not pray** as long as blood is visible and her missed prayers **do not have to be made up.**

rerequisites of Prayer

1. WEARING THE CORRECT CLOTHING :

A man must cover the front and back of his body between his navel and knees, as well as both his shoulders when praying. The garments must be loose and not transparent.

A woman must cover her entire body, except for her hands and face. The garments must be loose and not transparent.

2. ENSURING BODY, CLOTHING, AND PLACE OF PRAYER IS FREE FROM IMPURITIES

3. BEING IN A STATE OF PURITY

This means to have Wudu' (Ablution). The Prophet ﷺ said: **"Allah does not accept prayer without purity."**

(Muslim)

4. THE TIME FOR THE PRAYER HAS STARTED

Allah says: **"Verily, the prayer is enjoined on the believers at fixed times."**

5. FACING THE QIBLAH (DIRECTION OF THE KA'BAH)

Where ever a Muslim is in the world, they must face towards Makkah for prayer. There are special compasses designed to help you find the Qiblah direction.

6. PRAYING TOWARDS SOME SORT OF PARTITION (SUTRAH) WHEN ALONE AND IN AN OPEN AREA.

Haw to perform Salah (Step-by-Step)

PERFORMING THE FIRST RAK'AH (UNIT) OF PRAYER:

After facing the Qiblah the person should make an intention by thinking about the particular obligatory or optional prayer they intend to perform.

Step 1

In the standing position, raise both hands so that your finger tips are in line with the shoulders or ears. Your palms should be facing outward. Then say:

Allahu Akbar

(Allah is Greatest)

اللَّهُ أَكْبَرْ

Step 2

Place your hands on your chest, with the right hand over the left. Then say:

A'oothu billaahi minash-shaytanir-rajeem

(I seek refuge with Allah from Satan the accursed.)

أَعُوذُ بِاللَّهِ مِنَ الشَّيْطَانِ الرَّجِيمِ

Step 3 – Recite Surat Al-Fatiha

1 – Bismillaahir-rahmaanir-raheem

(In the name of Allah, the Most Beneficent, the Most Merciful)

بِسْمِ اللَّهِ الرَّحْمنِ الرَّحِيمِ

2 – Al-hamdu lillaahi rabbil 'aalameen

(Praise be to Allah the Lord of the Worlds)

الْحَمْدُ لِلَّهِ رَبِّ الْعَالَمِينَ

3 – Ar-rahmaanir-raheem

(The Most Beneficent, the Most Merciful)

الرَّحْمَنِ الرَّحِيمِ

4 – Maaliki yawmiddeen

(Master of the Day of Judgement)

مَالِكِ يَوْمِ الدِّينِ

5 – Iyyaaka na'budu wa iyyaaka nasta'een

(You alone we worship and in You alone we seek help)

إِيَّاكَ نَعْبُدُ وَإِيَّاكَ نَسْتَعِينُ

(Continued)

6 – Ihdinassiraatal mustaqeem

(Guide us to the straight path)

اهْدِنَا الصِّرَاطَ الْمُسْتَقِيمَ

7 – Siratallatheena an'amta 'alayhim

(The way of those whom You have favoured)

صِرَاطَ الَّذِينَ أَنْعَمْتَ عَلَيْهِمْ

Ghayril maghdoobi 'alayhim

(Not the way of those who have earned Your anger)

غَيْرِ الْمَغْضُوبِ عَلَيْهِمْ

Waladdaalleen

(Nor of those who have gone astray)

وَلَا الضَّالِّينَ

Aameen

(Oh Allah answer our prayer!)

آمين

Step 4

IF IT IS THE 1ST OR 2ND RAK'AH (UNIT):

Recite another chapter from the Qur'an. Refer to the end of this booklet for some short chapters from the Qur'an.

IF IT IS THE 3RD OR 4TH RAK'AH (UNIT):

Continue to Step 5 (Only the recitation of Surat Al-Fatiha is required)

Step 5

In the standing position, raise both hands as in Step 1. Then say:

Allahu Akbar

(Allah is Greatest)

اللهُ أَكْبَر

Step 6

You should now be in the bowing (rukoo') position. Say (3 *times*):

Subhaana rabbiyal 'atheem

(Glory be to my Lord the Supreme)

سُبْحَانَ رَبِّيَ الْعَظِيم

Step 7

Recite this as you come up from the bowing position.

Sami'-Allaahu liman hamidah

(Allah listens to the one who praises Him)

سَمِعَ اللَّهُ لِمَنْ حَمِدَه

Step 8

At this point you should stand with arms by your side.

Rabbanaa wa lakal hamd

(Our Lord، and to You belongs the praise)

رَبَّنَا وَلَكَ الْحَمْد

Step 9 – Prostration

Go into the prostration (sujood) positions seen below.
As you go into this position say:

Allahu Akbar

(Allah is Greatest)

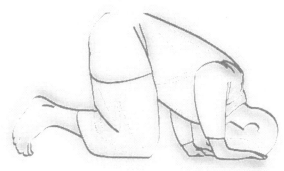

Then say (3 *times*): **Subhaana rabbiyal 'alaa**

(Glory be to my Lord Most High)

سُبْحَانَ رَبِّيَ الْأَعْلَى

IMPORTANT:

In the prostration position (sujood), ensure:

1. *The nose and forehead are touching the ground*
2. *The two palms are on the floor with fingers together*
3. *The two knees are on the floor*
4. *The toes of both feet are upright and not laying flat on the floor*

Step ١٠

While coming up to the sitting position say:

Allahu Akbar

(Allah is Greatest)

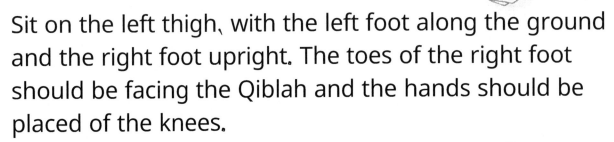

اللَّهُ أَكْبَر

Sit on the left thigh، with the left foot along the ground and the right foot upright. The toes of the right foot should be facing the Qiblah and the hands should be placed of the knees.

Then say (*3 times*):

Rabbighfirlee

(Oh Allah، forgive me)

رَبِّ اغْفِرْ لِي

Step ١١

Allahu Akbar

(Allah is Greatest)

اللَّهُ أَكْبَر

The first unit is now complete. Now you should complete the second/final rak'ah (unit).

Then say (*3 times*):

Subhaana rabbiyal 'alaa

(Glory be to my Lord Most High)

سُبْحَانَ رَبِّيَ الْأَعْلَى

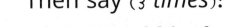

Haw to perform Salah (Step-by-Step)

PERFORMING THE SECOND OR FINAL RAK'AH (UNIT) OF PRAYER.

Step 1

Stand up and say:

Allahu Akbar

(Allah is Greatest)

اللَّهُ أَكْبَر

Step 2

Repeat Steps 3 to Step 11 from the first Rak'ah (unit) of prayer.

Step 3

After completing Step 11 from the first Rak'ah (unit) of prayer, say:

Allahu Akbar

اللَّهُ أَكْبَر

(Allah is Greatest)

Then go into the sitting position. At this point raise your index finger on your right hand. Now recite the following:

1- Attahiyyaatu lilaahi wassalawaatu wattayyibaatu

(All compliments, prayers and pure words are due to Allah)

التَّحِيَّاتُ لِلَّهِ وَالصَّلَوَاتُ وَالطَّيِّبَاتُ

2 - assalaamu 'alayka ay-yuhan-nabiyyu

(Peace be upon you Oh Prophet)

السَّلَامُ عَلَيْكَ أَيُّهَا النَّبِيُّ

3 - wa rahmatullaahi wabarakaatuh

(And the mercy of Allah and His blessings)

وَرَحْمَةُ اللَّهِ وَبَرَكَاتُهُ

Step 3
(Continued)

4 – assalaamu 'alaynaa wa 'alaa 'ibaadillaahissaliheen

(Peace be upon us and on the righteous slaves of Allah)

السَّلَامُ عَلَيْنَا وَعَلَى عِبَادِ اللَّهِ الصَّالِحِينَ

5 – Ash–hadu allaa ilaaha illallaah

(I bear witness that there is no God or deity worthy of worship except Allah)

أَشْهَدُ أَنْ لَا إِلَهَ إِلَّا اللَّهُ

6 – Wa ash–hadu anna Muhammadan 'abduhu wa rasooluh

(And I bear witness that Muhammad is His slave and Messenger)

وَأَشْهَدُ أَنَّ مُحَمَّدًا عَبْدُهُ وَرَسُولُهُ

Completing the Prayer

Step ١

١ – Allahumma salli 'ala Muhammad

(Oh Allah، send prayers upon Muhammad)

اللَّهُمَّ صَلِّ عَلَى مُحَمَّدٍ

٢ – wa 'ala aali Muhammad

(and upon the family of Muhammad)

وَعَلَى آلِ مُحَمَّدٍ

٣ – kamaa salyta 'ala Ibraheem

(as You sent prayers upon Ibrahim)

كَمَا صَلَّيْتَ عَلَى إِبْرَاهِيمَ

٤ – wa 'ala aali Ibraheem

(and upon the family of Ibrahim)

وَعَلَى آلِ إِبْرَاهِيمَ

innaka hameedun Majeed

(indeed You are praiseworthy، Most glorious)

إِنَّكَ حَمِيدٌ مَجِيدٌ

Step 1
(Continued)

6 – *wa baarik 'alaa Muhammad*

(and send Your blessings upon Muhammad)

وَبَارِكْ عَلَى مُحَمَّدٍ

7 – *wa 'alaa aali Muhammad*

(and upon the family of Muhammad)

وَعَلَى آلِ مُحَمَّدٍ

8 – *kamaa baarakta 'alaa Ibraheem*

(as You sent prayers upon Ibrahim)

كَمَا بَارَكْتَ عَلَى إِبْرَاهِيمَ

9 – *wa 'ala aali Ibraheem*

(and upon the family of Ibrahim)

وَعَلَى آلِ إِبْرَاهِيمَ

10 – *innaka hameedun Majeed*

(indeed You are praiseworthy, Most glorious)

إِنَّكَ حَمِيدٌ مَجِيدٌ

Step 2 – Right Side

Assalaamu 'alaykum wa rahmatullah

(May Allah's peace and mercy be upon you)

السَّلَامُ عَلَيْكُمْ

Step 3 – Left Side

Assalaamu 'alaykum wa rahmatullah

(May Allah's peace and mercy be upon you)

السَّلَامُ عَلَيْكُمْ

After Prayer – Supplication

1 – **Subhaan Allah** (Glory be to Allah) سُبْحَانَ اللَّهِ   Repeat **33 times**

2 – **Al-hamdu lillah** (Praise be to Allah) الْحَمْدُ لِلَّهِ   Repeat **33 times**

3 – **Allahu Akbar** (Allah is the greatest) اللَّهُ أَكْبَرُ   Repeat **33 times**

Short Qur'anic Chapters (Soorah)

Any of the following chapter may be recited after Surat al- Fatiha in the first two Rak'ah (units) of the prayer.

Surat Al-Kawthar (108)

سُوْرَةُ الْكَوْثَر (108)

Bismillaahir-rohmaanir-raheem

(In the name of Allah, the Most Beneficent, the Most Merciful)

1 – Innaa a'ataynaakal kawthar

(Indeed, We have granted you, (Oh Muhammad), al-Kawthar)

إِنَّا أَعْطَيْنَاكَ الْكَوْثَر

2 – Fasalli lirabika wanhar

(So pray to your Lord and sacrifice (for Him alone))

فَصَلِّ لِرَبِّكَ وَانْحَرْ

3 – Inna shaani'aka huwal abtar

(Indeed your enemy is the one cut off.)

إِنَّ شَانِئَكَ هُوَ الْأَبْتَرُ

Surat Al-Ikhlaas (112)

سُوْرَةُ الْإِخْلَاصِ (112)

Bismillaahir-rohmaanir-raheem

(In the name of Allah, the Most Beneficent, the Most Merciful)

بِسْمِ اللَّهِ الرَّحْمَٰنِ الرَّحِيمِ

1 – Qul huwallaahu ahad

(Say: He is Allah, (The) One)

قُلْ هُوَ اللَّهُ أَحَدٌ

2 – Allaahussamad

(Allah, the eternal Refuge {the one sought in times of difficulty and need})

اللَّهُ الصَّمَدُ

3 – Lam yalid walam yoolad

(He neither begets, nor is He born)

لَمْ يَلِدْ وَلَمْ يُولَدْ

4 – Walam yakullahu kufuwan ahad

(nor is there to Him any equivalent)

وَلَمْ يَكُنْ لَهُ كُفُوًا أَحَدٌ

Surat Al-Falaq (113)

سُوْرَةُ الْفَلَق

Bismillaahir-rohmaanir-raheem

(In the name of Allah, the Most Beneficent, the Most Merciful)

بِسْمِ اللَّهِ الرَّحْمَـٰنِ الرَّحِيمِ

1 – Qul a'oothu birabbil falaq

(Say: I seek refuge with the Lord of the daybreak)

قُلْ أَعُوذُ بِرَبِّ الْفَلَقِ

2 – Min sharri maa khalaq

(from the evil of what He has created)

مِنْ شَرِّ مَا خَلَقَ

3 – Wamin sharri ghasiqin ithaa waqab

(and from the evil of the darkening (night) as it comes with its darkness)

وَمِنْ شَرِّ غَاسِقٍ إِذَا وَقَبَ

4 – Wamin sharrin-naffaathaati fil'uqad

(and from the evil of the witchcraft when they blow in the knots)

وَمِنْ شَرِّ النَّفَّاثَاتِ فِي الْعُقَدِ

5 – Wamin sharri haasidin ithaa hasad

(and from the evil of the envier when he envies)

وَمِنْ شَرِّ حَاسِدٍ إِذَا حَسَدَ

Surat An-Nas (114)

سُـورة النَّاس (114)

Bismillaahir-rohmaanir-raheem

(In the name of Allah, the Most Beneficent, the Most Merciful)

بِسْمِ اللَّهِ الرَّحْمَنِ الرَّحِيمِ

1 – Qul a'oothu birabbinnas

(Say: I seek refuge with the Lord of Mankind)

قُلْ أَعُوذُ بِرَبِّ النَّاسِ

2 – Malikinnas

(The King of Mankind)

مَلِكِ النَّاسِ

3 – Ilaahinnas

(The God of Mankind)

إِلَهِ النَّاسِ

4 - Min sharril waswaasil khanaas

(From the evil of the whisperer who withdraws (when one remembers Allah))

مِنْ شَرِّ الْوَسْوَاسِ الْخَنَّاسِ

5 – Allathee yuwaswisu fee sudoorinnaas

(Who whispers in the breasts of mankind)

الَّذِي يُوَسْوِسُ فِي صُدُورِ النَّاسِ

6 – Minal jinnati wannas

(From among the jinn and mankind)

مِنَ الْجِنَّةِ وَالنَّاسِ

SUPPLICATIONS AFTER OBLIGATORY PRAYERS

1 – Astaghfirullah

(I ask Allah for forgiveness) (3 Times)

اَسْتَغْفِرُ اللَّه

2 – Alllhumma AntasSalam, Wa minkasSalam, Tabarakta yaa Dhal Jalali Wal'ikraam

(O Allah, You are As-Salam and from You is all peace, blessed are You, O Possessor of majesty and honour.' AS-Salam: The One Who is free from all defects and deficiencies).

اللّهُمَّ أَنْتَ السَّلامُ، وَمِنْكَ السَّلام، تَبارَكْتَ يا ذا الجَلالِ وَالإِكْرام

3 – La 'Ilaha 'Illallahu Whdahu La Shrika lahu,Lahul Mulku Wa Lahul Hamdu, Wa Huwa 'ala Kulli Shay'in Qadir, Allahumma Laa Man'a Lima A'tayta, Wa Laa Mu'tiya Limaa Mana'ta, Wa Laa Yanfa'u Dhal Jaddi Minkal AL-jadd

None has the right to be worshipped except Allah, alone, without partner, to Him belongs all sovereignty and praise and He is over all things omnipotent.O Allah, none can prevent what You have willed to bestow and none can bestow what You have willed to prevent, and no wealth or majesty can benefit anyone, as from You is all wealth and majesty

لا إلهَ إلاّ اللهُ وحدهُ لا شريكَ لهُ، لهُ المُلْكُ ولهُ الحَمْد، وهوَ على كلّ شيءٍ قَدير، اللّهُمَّ لا مانِعَ لِما أَعْطَيْت، ولا مُعْطِيَ لِما مَنَعْت، ولا يَنْفَعُ ذا الجَدّ مِنْكَ الجَد

4 – La Hawwla Wala Quwwata Illa Billah, La Ilaha Illallah, Wala Na'budu Illa 'iyahu, lahuNi'matu WalahulfadhluWalahuthThanaa' Ul Hasan, La 'ilaha 'illallah Mkhlisina LahudDiin Walaw Kariha Alkafirun

(There is no might nor power except with Allah, none has the right to be worshipped except Allah and we worship none except Him. For Him is all favour, grace, and glorious praise. None has the right to be worshipped except Allah and we are sincere in faith and devotion to Him although the disbelievers detest it)

لا حَوْلَ وَلا قوَّةَ إِلاَّ بِالله، لا إِلهَ إِلاَّ اللّهَ، وَلا نَعْبُدُ إِلاَّ إِيَّاه، لَهُ النّعْمَةُ وَلَهُ الفَضْلُ وَلَهُ الثّنَاءُ الحَسَن، لا إِلهَ إِلاَّ اللّهُ مخْلِصِينَ لَهُ الدِّينَ وَلَوْ كَرِهَ الكَافِرُون

Repeat Each 33 Times : (start reciting from the right)

7 – Allahu Akbar   **6 – Alhamdulillah**   **5 – subhanaAllah**

(Allah is the greatest) (Praise is to Allah) (Glory be to Allah)

سُبْحَانَ اللّه   اُلْحَمْدُ لِّله   سُبْحَانَ اللّه

And then say once :

La 'Ilaha 'Illallahu Whdahu La Shrika lahu,Lahul Mulku Wa Lahul Hamdu, Wa Huwa 'ala Kulli Shay'in Qadir

'None has the right to be worshipped except Allah, alone, without partner, to Him belongs all sovereignty and praise and He is over all things omnipotent

لا إلهَ إِلاَّ اللّهُ وحلهَ لاُ شَرِيكَ لهُ، لهُ المُلْكُ ولهُ الحَمْد، وهوَ على كلّ شَيءٍ قَلِير

Made in the USA
Middletown, DE
07 October 2023

40378058R10029